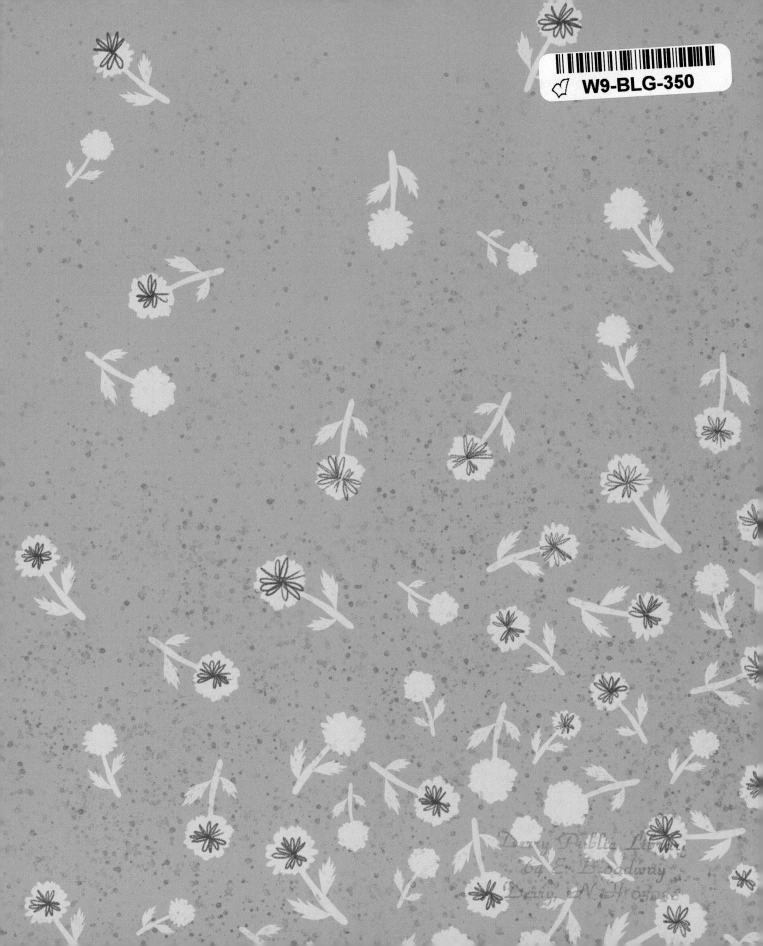

Text copyright © 2020 by Christine Baldacchino
Illustrations copyright © 2020 by Carmen Mok
Published in Canada and the USA in 2020 by Groundwood Books

Groundwood Books / House of Anansi Press
groundwoodbooks.com

We gratefully acknowledge for their financial support of our publishing
program the Canada Council for the Arts, the Ontario Arts Council and the
Government of Canada.

Canada Council   Conseil des Arts
for the Arts   du Canada

ONTARIO ARTS COUNCIL
CONSEIL DES ARTS DE L'ONTARIO
an Ontario government agency
un organisme du gouvernement de l'Ontario

With the participation of the Government of Canada   Canadä
Avec la participation du gouvernement du Canada

Library and Archives Canada Cataloguing in Publication

Title: Violet Shrink / Christine Baldacchino ; pictures by Carmen Mok.
Names: Baldacchino, Christine, author. | Mok, Carmen, illustrator.
Identifiers: Canadiana (print) 20190147504 | Canadiana (ebook) 20190147660 |
ISBN 9781773062051 (hardcover) | ISBN 9781773062068 (EPUB) |
ISBN 9781773063591 (Kindle)
Classification: LCC PS8603.A527 V56 2020 | DDC jC813/.6—dc23

The illustrations are in gouache, color pencil and graphite pencil.
Design by Michael Solomon
Printed and bound in Malaysia

For my beloved parents, Victor and
Violet Baldacchino, my wonderful
friend Dr. Rob Bittner, and my
loyal teddy bear, Junior — CB

To my best friend, Glenda Stafford,
who inspired my illustrations for
this book — CM

Violet Shrink

Christine Baldacchino   Pictures by Carmen Mok

Groundwood Books
House of Anansi Press
Toronto   Berkeley

Violet Shrink wears glasses like her father,
Victor, but has much more hair on her head.
She likes to listen to music through her purple
headphones and make her own comic books under
a tent of blankets in her room.

At school, when it's time to play outside, Violet likes to spend the time alone. She collects leaves, stones and dandelions to bring home and put on her window sill.

Violet likes birds, especially the birds that visit the feeder in her backyard every day.

There are things Violet doesn't like, too.

Violet doesn't like celery
in her soup.

She doesn't like brand-new crayons breaking the first time she uses them.

She doesn't like finding hairs on the kitchen table, even if they're her own.

And parties.

Violet really doesn't like parties.

Her father reminds her that she
likes cake, music and games, and those
are all things you can find at parties.

Violet wants to tell her father that
while she likes all those things, she
doesn't like them all at the same time.

Being around a lot of people makes
her palms sweat. Sometimes her
ears feel hot or her stomach aches.
Sometimes she squeezes her teeth
together so hard that her head hurts.

Violet loves her father very much, even though he often gets her to go to a party by using a word she's never heard before. A word like "reception" or "function" or "potluck." He tells her to play with the other children and say hello to all the grown-ups.

But Violet just wishes she could stay home in her tent with her purple headphones and her comic books.

One day, while she is picking celery out of her soup, Violet's father tells her that they have been invited to a little shindig for Cousin Char.

When they arrive at her cousin's house, Violet is horrified to discover that it is a birthday party.

Violet spends the entire time hiding under the kitchen table. She imagines she is a shark, smooth and silver, with a hundred sharp, white teeth. She swims in circles and loop-di-loops, hunting for sandwiches to eat.

Her ears don't feel hot anymore because sharks don't have ears that stick out the way hers do, and her palms aren't sweating because sharks don't have hands.

Just two weeks later, Violet's father tells her they are going to an anniversary bash for Auntie Marlene and Uncle Leli. The word "bash" reminds her of loud things like drums, fireworks, or pots and pans banging together.

Sure enough, "bash" turns out to be another word for party.

"Make sure you say hello to everyone, Violet.
And play with your cousins," her father says when
they get there. "No hiding under tables today,
okay?"

Violet wipes her sweaty palms on her pants and
squeezes her teeth together until her head hurts.

She doesn't hide under a table. Instead, she sits quietly at the top of the stairs where no one can see her, legs dangling between the bannisters.

She imagines she is a snake, gold and green as a dandelion, wrapped around the branch of a very tall tree. Balanced on a branch below is the chocolatiest slice of chocolate cake...

Violet knows her father isn't trying to be mean. He wants her to go to parties for the same reason he keeps putting celery in her soup — he thinks it is good for her.

But when Violet's father tells her that the Shrink family reunion is coming up, she silently goes to her room.

There will be a lot more relatives than usual, and more
people means more voices. Louder voices. Uncle Louie will
play his accordion, and Uncle Joe will do his weird moose-
stuck-in-the-mud dance, and all of Violet's aunts will
laugh so loud she'll feel it in the pit of her stomach.

Violet isn't hungry anymore, not even for dessert. All
she wants to do is crawl into her blanket tent, put her
headphones on and draw pictures of bats. But that will
have to wait.

"Dad, I have an important thing to say," Violet says as he is tucking her into bed for the night.

"Okay," he says, putting on his listening-for-real face.

"I don't like parties." Violet's stomach gives an unpleasant little flutter. "Or shindigs. Or bashes. Or get-togethers. Or gatherings. I don't like any of those things."

Her dad starts to say what he always says. "You like cake, don't you? And you like music, don't you? And you like games, don't you?"

"Yes," Violet replies. "But not all at the same time!"

She tells him how her stomach hurts, and her palms sweat, and her ears get hot. Her father keeps his listening-for-real face on the whole time, which makes the words come more easily.

"And I don't like celery in my soup," she adds. "I don't think I ever will."

"What if I leave out the celery but put in extra carrots?" he asks.

"I don't hate carrots," she replies.

"Well, that solves that. Now what are we going to do about all these parties?"

"I think I know," Violet says, glancing at her blanket tent.

The Shrink family reunion ends up being quite the wingding, as Violet's father would say.

As expected, Uncle Louie plays the accordion, and Uncle Joe teaches all her cousins how to do his weird moose-stuck-in-the-mud dance. Everyone laughs loudly, and someone breaks a big, ugly lamp that Auntie Mary says she never liked anyway.

But for the very first time, Violet's stomach doesn't ache, her palms don't sweat, and her ears don't feel hot.

Because as the Shrink family parties late into the evening, Violet sits under the dessert table — purple headphones over her ears, a pile of comic books in her lap and a smile on her face.

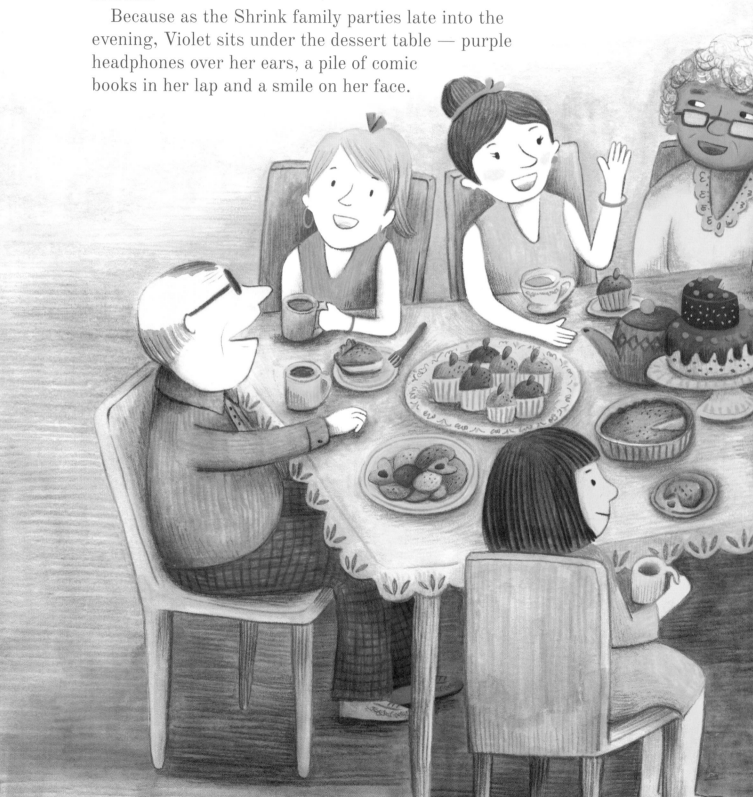

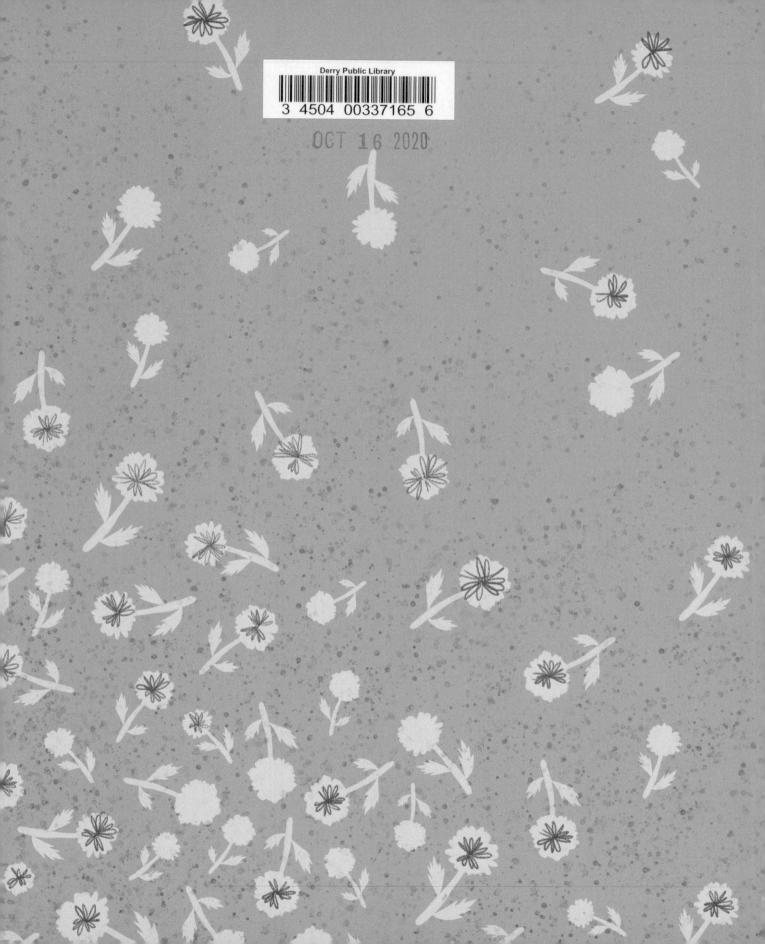